Junkyard Dan

Stolen?

D1561692

NOX PRESS

books for that extra kick to give you more power

www.NoxPress.com

Also by Elise Leonard:

The **JUNKYARD DAN** series: (*Nox Press*)

1. Start of a New Dan
2. Dried Blood
3. Stolen?
4. Gun in the Back
5. Plans
6. Money for Nothing
7. Stuffed Animal
8. Poison, Anyone?
9. A Picture Tells a Thousand Dollars
10. Wrapped Up
11. Finished
12. Bloody Knife
13. Taking Names and Kicking Assets
14. Mercy

THE SMITH BROTHERS (a series): (*Nox Press*)

1. All for One   5. Master Plan
2. When in Rome
3. Get a Clue
4. The Hard Way

A LEEG OF HIS OWN (a series): (*Nox Press*)

1. Croaking Bullfrogs, Hidden Robbers
2. 20,000 LEEGS Under the C
3. Failure to Lunch
4. Hamlette

The **AL'S WORLD** series: (*Simon & Schuster*)

Book 1: Monday Morning Blitz
Book 2: Killer Lunch Lady
Book 3: Scared Stiff
Book 4: Monkey Business

Junkyard Dan

Stolen?

Elise Leonard

books for that extra kick to give you more power

www.NoxPress.com

Leonard, Elise
Junkyard Dan series / Stolen?
ISBN: 978-0-9815694-2-0

Printed in the U.S.A.
First Nox Press printing: March 2008
Second Nox Press printing: December 2008
Third Nox Press printing: December 2009

NOX PRESS
books for that extra kick to give you more power

For my readers,

Thanks for all the great responses.
I'm so glad you're enjoying
the JUNKYARD DAN series.

Hugs to you all!

~Elise

Chapter 1

It had been a long day and a long night. But a lot of good came out of my troubles.

I had no idea what I'd find. At first I was scared. I didn't want to know.

A blood-covered car? That couldn't be good!

How could it?

But I'd kept at it. Kept searching. And found out what had happened.

I'd solved the mystery of the bloody Honda Civic. Me. Dan Corbett. All by myself.

I had no one to be impressed by what I'd done.

I had no one who cared.

So it didn't seem like it counted.

But if you'd ask me? It *did* count. And I was

pleased.

The whole thing wasn't as bad as I'd thought it was going to be.

I mean, sure, I'd wanted peace. Peace and quiet.

That's why I'd moved from New York. To live a simple life.

A quiet life.

But that's not quite how things worked out.

At first I was annoyed. Annoyed that I couldn't just start my simple life.

My simple life as a junkyard owner. A junkyard owner in the middle of nowhere!

In quiet Peaceville. Peaceville, Florida.

I mean, how action-packed can a place named Peaceville be?

Life couldn't be hectic in Peaceville.

At least I didn't think it could be. Didn't think it *would* be, either.

But so far? It wasn't very peaceful.

Those bloody parts sure snarled things up. I'd thought I was really in a mess when *that*

Stolen?

happened.

But, in the end, it had all worked out.

So in a way, I was glad I'd gotten involved. Even if it was a pain in my butt.

In fact, in the end? It was kind of nice.

A lot of people could start healing now.

I knew how powerful healing was.

You see, *I* was healing.

Well, trying to. But it was hard.

Every now and then my mind would wander. Wander to thoughts of Patti.

She was my wife. My reason for living. My whole life.

But then she left me.

Just took off. Took everything I owned.

She left with the 23-year-old roofer I'd hired to fix our roof.

I know I should hate her. But I don't.

Deep down I miss her. Really deep down.

But sometimes? It bubbles to the top. And when it does? The pain hits hard.

This was one of those times.

I was driving back to Peaceville. Alone.

Nothing to keep me company but my thoughts.

At first I thought of the family I had brought together.

Well, families.

I'd brought Seth and Dee Dee and their baby together. That was one family.

I'd brought Seth's parents back together with Seth. That was the second family I'd helped.

And I'd helped Dee Dee's parents fix something they should have fixed long ago.

They were the third family I'd helped.

So it was a good thing I followed through on the bloody Honda parts.

But on the long drive home to Peaceville? I was alone. And thinking about being alone.

And thinking of Patti.

Which made me feel even *more* alone.

Mostly because I had no one with which to share all these "good deed" feelings I was having.

Chapter 2

I was cruising down the highway. Lost in thought.

Heading for home.

The miles were passing like a long black ribbon. Black ribbon stretched before me. And black ribbon filled the rear view mirror.

It seemed endless.

I was trying not to think about Patti. But I was.

You know how that is. Like when someone says, "Don't think about zebras!"

All you can think about? *Zebras*!

Not that you'd ever think about zebras. You probably hadn't thought about zebras for years. (If ever!)

But now? Now that someone told you *not* to think about zebras? That's all you could think about.

So by *not* trying to think about Patti? That's all I could think about.

Luckily, my cell phone rang.

I picked it up off the seat and answered.

"Dan Corbett," I barked into the phone.

"Whoa. Dude. Lighten up! You don't have to be so formal."

It was Bubba. I could sort of tell by his voice. He didn't sound like any of the Wall Street guys I used to work with.

Plus, he was the only one with my cell number.

At least the only one who would call me.

"Sorry," I replied. "Old habits die hard."

That made Bubba laugh. "Yeah, well, you're not a big stockbroker dude now. You own a junkyard. Try to act like it."

Now *I* was laughing.

Guess I should cut it back a notch. Or two. Or a thousand.

Stolen?

"Want to call back and I'll try again?" I asked Bubba.

"Nah," Bubba said with good cheer. "You're a smart guy. You'll learn soon enough," he added.

In my mind, I could see that grin of his.

My old Aunt Sue would say Bubba had a "devilish grin." She'd also say he had a twinkle in his eye that showed he was up to something.

True, Bubba had a devilish streak. But he was a good guy. And if he was up to no good? Well, maybe so. But it didn't seem in his nature to hurt anyone.

Well, except for those sandwiches he kept in his garage's vending machine. But let's not go there.

"So what can I do for you?" I asked Bubba.

"That guy's back," he said.

"What guy?" I asked.

"The guy who wants to buy a car from the yard."

"Oh. Yeah. Now I remember," I said.

Bubba had called me the day before. He'd said

some man came in and wanted to buy a car to restore with his son.

"What's up?" I asked.

"He's back. He really wants that car," Bubba said.

"The one with the VIN numbers scratched off. Right?" I asked.

"Right," Bubba said.

I was almost back at the junkyard. I only had about ten more minutes to go.

"Look. I'll be back in ten minutes," I told Bubba.

"So what do you want me to tell the guy?" Bubba asked.

I had no clue. "I don't know. I'm new to this whole junkyard thing. Remember?"

"Yeah, I remember," Bubba said with a laugh. "Plus, it's not hard to tell. You really don't know your butt from your elbow, do you?!"

If anyone else had said that? I'd take offense. And probably would be ticked off. But this was Bubba. And to tell you the truth? I liked that we joked around like this.

It was nice having a friend. A real friend.

One who I felt had my back.

"When it comes to the junkyard? You're right, Bubba. I don't know what I'm doing," I said honestly.

That made Bubba laugh.

"Yeah," he said. "But you're learning."

I smiled at that.

"How about you take the guy to Hilda's diner and get some of her great pie? It's on me," I said.

"Sounds like a plan," Bubba said. "Thanks."

"Oh wait," I said. "But what about your garage?"

"I'll leave a note on the door," Bubba said with a chuckle. "My momma didn't raise a fool. Free pie? You don't have to ask *me* twice!"

"Can you do that?" I asked. "You know. Just leave a note on the garage's door?"

"This is Peaceville, Dan!" Bubba said with a laugh. "Whoever shows up at the shop will come find me at Hilda's diner."

Chapter 3

I drove up to Hilda's diner. I parked two spaces from the door.

It still got to me that I could park so easily in Peaceville. New York City was so different!

I stopped myself from locking up the car. It was a habit I no longer had to worry about.

When I walked through the door, Hilda was right there.

"So? Did you find out about the blood in the car?" she asked.

"Sure did," I told her.

"Hey," Bubba called from a booth. "Leave Dan alone, Hilda. We've got stuff to discuss here!"

It was kind of nice having all this attention.

Stolen?

I wasn't used to having people around who cared. About anything!

Patti had only cared to know how much money I was bringing in. She never asked about my day.

That was fine with me, though. I wasn't too thrilled with how my days went when I was a stockbroker anyhow.

But now? Now that I'd actually done something nice? It felt good to be able to share it.

"Yes," I said to Hilda. "I found out. But it wasn't what we'd thought."

"What was it?" she asked. "What happened? Enquiring minds want to know, you know!"

That made me laugh.

"I'll tell you all about it some other time," I said. "Let me handle this first. Okay?"

"Yeah, I guess," she replied.

I slid into the booth next to Bubba.

A man was sitting across from Bubba. I assumed he was my new customer.

I held out my hand. "Hi. I'm Dan," I said.

We shook hands.

"Roger," he said with a nod. "I'm Roger Strands."

"Nice to meet you," I said. "So what can I do for you?"

Hilda came over with a cup of coffee and a piece of apple pie. With vanilla ice cream on top. Of course.

She knew how I liked it.

I smiled up at Hilda as she set the food before me. "Thanks, Hilda."

She winked in response. "Need anything else?"

"Nope. This is just perfect. Thanks," I told her.

I looked back at Roger Strands.

"Now. What can I do for you?" I asked him again.

"My son is growing up fast. Too fast for my taste, if you'd ask me. Soon he'll be off on his own," Roger Strands said.

"That's a good thing. Isn't it?" Bubba asked the man.

He shrugged then nodded slowly. "Yes. I guess. Maybe. But I miss spending time with him.

Stolen?

Now he's into his friends… girls… cars. You know how it is."

I nodded.

"Friends, girls and cars? I *still* know how that is!" Bubba said with a chuckle.

Roger smiled. "I miss him. I want him back for a little while longer. Before he leaves for good."

I got where he was going with this.

"So you figure you'll restore a car together," I said with a grin. "Good plan."

Roger smiled. "He's always loved the first generation Camaros. You know, the 1967, the '68 and the '69 model."

"What's not to love about *those*?" Bubba said with feeling.

We all laughed.

Then Roger got serious. "I want that '69 Camaro in your yard. It'll be a great project for my son and me to work on," Roger said.

I nodded.

Even though I didn't have a son, I knew what he wanted to do. I knew how hard it was to give up someone you love.

I felt for the man.

"I can't sell it without a VIN number," I said gently.

"And he can't sell it at *all*, if it's been stolen," Bubba added.

"But I'll do what I can to find out *why* the VIN numbers were scratched off. And if I *can* sell it—it's yours," I told Roger.

Roger's smile said it all.

Now I just had to find out why those VIN numbers were scratched off. And *that* wasn't going to be easy!

Chapter 4

I got home and unpacked. Then I played with the dogs for a while.

Bubba fed them while I was gone. But I could tell they wanted to play a little.

Fetch was their favorite game.

I'd bought them quite a few balls. That way, they wouldn't fight over them.

I think I threw five hundred times. At *least*!

"Okay, guys. Enough playing. I've got to find that '69 Camaro. Anyone know where it is?"

I looked at my pack of dogs. They all looked back at me.

But not one of them answered.

I was glad of that. A talking dog would have

freaked me out.

So I went looking for the '69 Camaro. The one with the scratched off VIN numbers.

Of course the dogs came with me.

I liked the company. They walked beside me, quietly. They kept running around or went off to wander. But they always came back to check where I was.

They didn't bark. Just walked with me. It was nice.

The long walk cleared my head.

I could think as I walked. Enjoyed it, really.

It was so peaceful and quiet. And the dogs by my side were pleasant company.

I didn't have to amuse them. And they didn't have to amuse me. It was just nice.

It allowed me to think about things.

Like the Camaro.

I had *no* idea how I'd track down the owner. Not without a VIN.

I'd have to look through any records that old Junkyard Dan had left. Maybe I'd find something there. But I doubted it.

The records in the office were not very good. *Or* complete. In fact, there were few records there at all. And the ones that *were* there? They were mostly notes on matchbook covers or napkins.

Not too official. And they didn't make much sense.

The old Junkyard Dan wasn't much for keeping records. That's for sure.

I kept walking around the yard. I knew I'd get to the Camaro sooner or later.

It was okay that I hadn't come across it yet. I was getting a good idea of what was in the yard with this walk.

I was on the east side of the yard when I spotted the old Camaro.

It was faded, and rusted in parts. It looked old and worn. Tired. But you could see it was something else in its day.

It must've been a real beauty.

The lines were unlike any car ever made before or after. The first generation Camaros really were a piece of art.

Whoever designed them should've been proud.

As I came upon the car, I heard a groan.

"Get your dog germs off me!" someone said with fake anger. Then he chuckled.

It was a low rumble. From deep within his chest.

"Is someone there?" I said aloud. I knew full well someone was there, but didn't know what else to say.

The dogs were gathering around an old VW bus.

I walked to the bus, wondering what I'd find. *Who* I'd find, really.

There was a cup of something on top of the VW bus. It was still steaming.

Whoever was there had not been there for long.

Chapter 5

"Hello?" a deep voice said slowly.

"Hello?" I answered.

"Dan?" the deep voice said. "It doesn't sound like you."

"It's not me. Well, I mean, it *is* me. But not the Dan you think I am."

A grisly old man came out of the van.

"Who are you?" he asked.

"I was wondering the same thing," I said.

"You don't know who you are?" he asked. "That Dan! Always taking in strays. Stray cats. Stray dogs. Stray people. This place is turning into a zoo!" he muttered.

"I know who *I* am, I just don't know who *you*

are," I said.

"Where's Dan?" the man asked.

I noticed that he'd never answered my question about who he was.

"Dan passed away," I said.

That got a response. The man paled.

He was a gruff, old African American man. But his skin had turned pale with the news of Dan's death.

"I'm so sorry to hear that," the man said.

He looked at me and his old eyes were watery.

"I didn't know him," I said gently.

"You missed a good thing," the man said gently.

"I could tell," I said softly. I'd meant it, too.

I wondered if this man was related to Junkyard Dan. They were both quite old and of the same race.

"I'm Miles," the man said. He offered his hand.

"Dan," I said, shaking hands.

"Really?" he asked with a crooked smile.

I grinned. "Really."

Stolen?

"So what brings you here?" the old man asked.

"I own the place," I said simply. "What brings *you* here?"

I think he blushed. But I wasn't sure.

"Dan and I were old friends," Miles said. He looked off into the distance. Like he was remembering something. "He let me come here whenever I wanted to. Or needed to."

I didn't know what he'd meant by that last thing. But I didn't have time to ask.

"Dan and I go way back!" he said. Then he stopped talking. "I mean, we *went* way back."

He shook his head and sighed heavily.

"I can't believe he's gone," Miles said sadly.

"Yes," I said. "I'm sorry you didn't know."

Miles nodded. I could tell he was fighting back tears. He must have been close to Dan.

"He let me stay here," Miles said as he looked into the distance again. "Now where will I go?"

I didn't know what to say. The man looked homeless. I didn't want to take the guy's home away. Nor did I want to make him feel bad by asking if he had somewhere else to go.

"What was your deal with Dan?" I asked him.

"He would let me come and go. I didn't really bother him much. Only came when I had nowhere else to go." He looked around. "Having this place was a blessing for me."

Again, his eyes filled with tears.

"Look," I told him. "I'd like to keep the deal in place. If it's okay with you, that is."

His old, weary eyes flashed to mine. "Are you sure?" he asked.

I nodded. "Yes, I'm sure. I could use some help around here."

That seemed to make him nervous. "But I come and go. I'm like a rolling stone. I don't like to stay in one place very long," he said.

"That's okay," I said.

"It is? I want you to know the truth about me," he said with great sadness.

I shook my head. "Miles, we all have skeletons in the closet. You don't have to tell me anything you don't want to tell me. In fact, for now? Let's

Stolen?

just get to know each other for who we are now. Okay?"

That seemed to lighten his load.

He smiled widely. "Sure thing, boss."

"Hey. I'm no one's boss. I gave all that up when I bought the junkyard," I told him.

He chuckled at that.

It seems we *both* had baggage. *And* issues.

"So what are you doing now?" Miles asked me.

I pointed to the old '69 Camaro. "Looking into that car," I told him. "The VIN numbers are scratched off."

Miles smiled widely. "Yup. There's a story behind *that* old car."

I scratched my chin. "Sure wish I knew what it was."

"Maybe I could help," Miles said.

I took a shot in the dark. "Do you know the story behind the car?" I asked.

I wasn't expecting an answer.

"It just so happens that I do," Miles said with a smile. His smile looked like that of a Cheshire cat.

Chapter 6

"You *know* something?" I asked Miles.

He smiled widely. Then he winked. "I know a *lot* of things."

"About the *car*," I said. I pointed to the old Camaro.

"Sure do," he said. "It's a 1969 Camaro."

I rolled my eyes. "I already *knew* that," I said.

"It only had one owner," he added.

"Now *that*, I didn't know."

Miles grunted and nodded. "Didn't think so."

"Do you know who owned it?" I asked.

Miles shrugged. "I met the man."

"Do you remember his name?" I asked.

He shook his head. "Nope. Sorry. But I do

remember his face."

That didn't help me much.

"I remember that day well," he said with a smile. "But only because it was so funny."

"Funny?"

"Yeah," Miles said. "This guy comes in. *With* his wife." Then Miles whistled low and long. "Whoo-ee, she was easy on the eyes! You know what I mean?"

I nodded and smiled. "Yes, I know what you mean."

"She could have been a pin-up girl. And I'm not talking the trashy stuff you do with women now-a-days. I'm talking about the pin-ups of the '40s. You remember those?" he asked me.

"No. Sorry. I wasn't around then," I said with a crooked grin.

"Too bad. You really missed something," he said.

He had a faraway look. As though he could see the pin-up girls clearly in his mind's eye.

"I hate to break into your trip down memory

lane. But do you think you could remember anything else about this couple?" I asked Miles.

He thought about my question.

"Oh. I've got something," he said with a warm smile.

"What?" I asked.

"That guy sure did love that woman!" Miles said easily. Then he chuckled. "He would have done *anything* for that woman."

Again, this wasn't helpful.

"Ever love a woman that way?" Miles asked me.

I didn't feel like sharing. Or going into it. But he asked a question, and I felt I should answer it.

"Yes. I did," I admitted.

"And was it worth it?" Miles asked.

I thought about that. "For a while."

"But then it went bad?" he asked. He looked like he knew about that. Looked like he knew firsthand about love gone bad.

"You could say that," I said with a shrug.

I didn't want Miles to see how stupid I'd been.

Stolen?

Or how Patti had hurt me.

"That's too bad," he said quietly.

I nodded. I had nothing to add to that.

We stood in silence for a few seconds.

"It's usually worth it, though," he said gently.

"Yes," I agreed. "I guess."

There was another long pause.

"You know? I think I remember where that man's wife used to work," Miles said.

He turned to me and laughed.

"It was a long time ago, mind you," he added.

"That's okay," I said.

"I figure you could start looking there," he said.

I smiled. "It's the only lead I've got."

"So I guess it's the perfect place to start," Miles said. That low rumble of a laugh came up from his chest.

Chapter 7

"You never finished your story," I told Miles.

"What story?" he asked.

"You said that you remembered the day you met the man who dropped off the Camaro."

"I do," he said.

"You said it was a funny day," I reminded him.

"It was," he said.

"Care to tell me *why*?" I asked.

I was starting to lose patience.

"Why what?" he asked.

"Why the *day* was *funny*!" I said a little too loudly.

Miles laughed.

"I was just playing with you, Dan. You really

need to relax a little," he said in his deep voice.

"Very funny," I said.

"Hey, I may be old, but I'm not stupid," he said with a grin.

"Okay. I'll try to relax. Now would you *please* tell me why that day was so funny?"

Miles closed his eyes to recall the day. Then laughter bubbled out of him. "That man was here under duress. *Extreme* duress."

I didn't get what he was trying to say. "What does that mean?" I asked.

"It means, he didn't want to give up that car."

"So why *did* he?" I asked Miles.

"Because that pretty little lady of his was making him."

"Why?" I asked.

"That's what was so funny!" Miles said with a chuckle. "This drop dead gorgeous woman was nagging the man. She kept saying, 'You love that car more than you love me!'"

Miles laughed some more.

"Then *he* kept saying, 'No I don't,'" Miles

explained.

He was laughing hard. Tears were rolling down his old, wrinkled face.

"Then she would say, 'Then just give it up. Just like that. Give it up. For *me*!'"

Miles had done the woman's voice sounding like a woman. He even pranced around the yard. Like he was wearing a skirt and high heels. He was copying the woman from long ago.

That made me laugh.

"Let me get this straight," I said. "They were having problems. Like most couples do. But it was a *car* that came between them?"

Miles hooted with laughter. "I know. It's absurd, isn't it?" He slapped his knee and laughed some more.

"Not as absurd as you trying to act like a young woman," I said.

I pointed to his feet. He was still up on his tippy toes. Like he was still wearing high heels.

He kept laughing. And tears kept running from his eyes.

Stolen?

"It was *too* funny! She kept saying that he loved that car more than her."

"Did he?" I asked.

"If he *did*, he was an idiot!" Miles said with trouble. He was trying to stop laughing.

"I know. I know. The woman was hot," I said.

"Not hot. *Pretty*. Beautiful. She was the prettiest thing I'd seen in these parts in a long while. You young people with the 'hot' this and 'hot' that."

He looked at me and tilted his head. Like he didn't understand me at all.

"It's not always about sex, you know. It's about mystery. Intrigue. Decency. Class. You kids today. You have no class. You have no subtlety. Nothing is refined. There's no nuance. It's all just out there. Hanging right out in the open. In your face."

"Can't handle it, Pops?" I joked.

"No. It's not that. You kids don't know what you're missing. The wondering. The question. The promise."

He was trying to tell me something. And I think I knew what he meant.

"You mean like all the ads today are blatantly about sex?"

"Yes," he said. "Today, *everything* seems to be about sex."

He had a point.

We stood there, each with our own thoughts.

He was most likely thinking about the days of yesterday.

I was thinking about the days of today.

"Want me to take you to where the lady worked?" Miles asked.

Chapter 8

We were driving to where the woman worked.

"You realize we're going to look like idiots," I said.

"What makes you say that?" Miles asked.

He brushed at the smudges of dirt on his clothes.

I didn't want him to feel badly about what he was wearing. Or what he looked like. It probably wasn't his fault that he was homeless. Plus, I hadn't meant it literally.

"I didn't mean that we'd *look* like idiots. I meant that we'd *seem* like idiots," I corrected.

"Why?" Miles asked. "Because we're going in there to ask about a lady?"

"A lady whose *name* we don't know," I said. "How are we going to go in there and ask about a lady, if we don't know her *name*?!"

Miles laughed.

"What are we going to do? Say, 'Hey! Do you know the name of that lady who worked here a long time ago?'"

Miles laughed harder.

"We're going to look like half-wits! Doesn't that *bother* you?" I asked Miles.

He was still laughing.

"First of all," Miles said. "Why do *you* care what these people think of you?"

He had a point.

"You'll never see them again," he added.

He had another point.

"And, you didn't *see* this woman," Miles explained. "If there's one person in the building who was there when *she* was? They'll remember her. Take my word."

I didn't know if what he said was true or not. But it was worth a shot. Plus, I had no other leads.

Stolen?

So it was my *only* shot.

When we got to the door of the building, I yanked it open.

"After you," I said to Miles.

He motioned with his hand. "No. Please. You first. Age before beauty."

The man was a character. But not without charm.

He had plenty of charm. That's for sure.

There was a young receptionist sitting in the center of the room.

"May I help you?" she asked.

"Yes, we're looking... ah, for an old, ah... woman," I said.

Miles elbowed me out of the way.

"Please excuse my friend," he said. "He doesn't know what he's talking about."

Miles threw me a dirty look.

"We're looking for a woman who worked here many years ago. Possibly twenty-five or thirty years ago."

The girl popped her gum. "I wouldn't know

about that," she said. She popped two more bubbles. "I wasn't even born then."

"Yes," Miles said with a warm smile. "Most likely not. But is there someone here who might be able to help us?"

"You can try personnel," she said.

"Okay," Miles said. "Please tell us how to get there."

"Down that hall," she pointed over her shoulder. "Go to the end. Turn left. Then go about three doors down. Maybe four. Anyhow. Then you'll make a right. Go through that office. Through the next office, too. Then hang a right. You'll come to another hallway. Go down there. Then, the fifth door on the right hand side? That's the personnel office. But go to the second office on the left. She's nicer. The guy in the first office is mean."

She had to be kidding! Right?

With those directions? I already had a pain thumping in my head.

I looked at Miles. He was smiling and nodding.

Stolen?

"Okay," he said to the girl.

"You got all that?" she asked.

She was kidding again. Right?

"Sure did," Miles said.

Was *he* kidding?!

"Isn't there an easier way to get there?" I asked the girl.

She popped her gum before answering. "Nope. Sorry."

"It's okay," Miles said. "I got it."

He pointed to his gray-hair covered temple. Then he tapped it a few times.

"It's all up here," he said with a grin. "Follow me."

"I will," I told him. "Because she lost me after she said, 'go to the end.'"

"That was the second step," Miles said with a chuckle.

"Yeah!" I said. "The second step of about *fifteen.*"

"Just follow me," Miles said.

I did.

Dang, he was smart! I would've needed a GPS system to get to the personnel office in this place.

"Don't you think they should put the personnel office closer to the front?" I asked Miles.

"Why?" he asked back.

"So new people could get there easily," I explained. "Can you imagine going for a job interview? And having to find the personnel office in this place?" I asked him.

"Maybe they use this to weed out the people who can't follow directions," Miles said.

"Well," I said. "I'd be weeded out!"

That made Miles laugh. "You're funny, Dan."

Too bad I wasn't *trying* to be!

Chapter 9

By the time we got to personnel? My head was spinning.

"How did you *get* us here?" I asked Miles.

He shrugged. "Simple. I followed that girl's directions."

"What are you? Brilliant or something?" I asked.

"I've been called worse," Miles said with a smile.

I looked around the personnel office.

The woman sitting there was about twenty years old. Maybe twenty-two. Tops.

"Hello," Miles said warmly. "May we ask some questions about a former employee?"

"That depends," she said.

"On what?" Miles asked.

"On whether I'm allowed to give out the information you want," she said.

And this was the *nice* one of the department?

I guess I'd been spoiled. In the last place I worked? Everyone called me "sir" and ran around trying to make me happy.

Here? No one called me sir.

No one thought I was important.

And no one cared if I was happy.

I guess this was how most people were treated.

It wasn't very nice.

"We're looking for a woman who used to work here," Miles said.

"What's her name?" the young woman asked.

"Well," Miles said with a grin and a shrug. "That's the problem."

She stared at Miles as if he had two heads.

"We don't *know* her name," I said. I'd used my best business voice. But she was clearly not impressed.

Stolen?

"How can I look her up, if you don't know her name?" she asked.

"We were hoping you might be able to track her down," Miles tried again.

"I can't track her *down*, if I *don't* know her *name*!" Her voice was raised now.

She was starting to get a little attitude.

If you asked me? It was a little early to start yelling.

We should've been able to ask at *least* two more stupid questions before the yelling began.

Whatever happened to the saying, "The customer is always right"?

True, we weren't customers. But we still should get a *little* leeway before getting yelled at.

"Look, dudes," she spat out. "I don't get paid enough for this."

The guy from the next office came in. "What's going on in here?" he asked.

"We're trying to find the name of a former employee of yours," I told him.

The man looked at the young woman.

41

Her eyes were angry.

I was shocked to see that she shot daggers at him. "You want to mind your own business?" she asked her co-worker.

He looked from the woman to Miles.

"Please," he said to us. "Come into *my* office. Maybe I can help you."

We followed him into his office.

According to my office count? And according to the girl at the front desk? This was supposed to be the *mean* guy.

I looked at Miles.

He grinned and looked back at me. Then he shrugged.

We waited for the man to get behind his desk.

"So how can I help you?" he asked.

"We're looking for a woman who used to work here a long time ago," Miles said.

"And her name is?" he asked. He was reaching for a file cabinet.

"We don't know her name," I said.

He stopped reaching. "Oh," he said. "That

might be a problem."

"I don't mean to be rude, but is there someone more, um, *experienced* working here?"

"I'm the head of the department," he said.

"You *are*?" I asked. I looked at the crazy young woman in the next office.

"I know," the man said. "I'd *love* to fire her. She's rude and lazy. Not to mention that she can get nasty when provoked. But I can't fire her."

"We didn't provoke her," Miles said in our defense.

The man nodded. "I'm sure not." Then he made a face. "She can get nasty even when she's *not* provoked."

"Then why can't you fire her?" I asked.

"She's my daughter."

"Oh," Miles and I said together.

"She wouldn't care if I fired her. She'd most likely be happy about it. But her mother? My wife?"

Miles held up his hand. "You don't have to explain. We understand. Enough said."

"Thanks," he said with a grimace.

We stood there staring at each other. All three of us.

"What about an old timer?" Miles finally said.

"What?" the man asked.

"Do you have an old timer working here?" Miles asked.

"There's a guy in the shipping department who has been here a *long* time."

"May we speak with him?" I asked.

The man shrugged. "Sure. I'll take you there. This place can seem like a maze if you don't know the place."

I looked at Miles and made a face. "See? Even *he* knows it's hard to get around in this place."

Miles tried to look innocent. "I didn't have any trouble."

But then he smiled and his eyes twinkled.

"Oh, be quiet," I told Miles as we followed the guy through the tangle of offices.

Chapter 10

"We're looking for a woman who used to work here. We think it was maybe about twenty-five or thirty years ago," I said to the older man.

"She had long red hair," Miles added. "And a figure, well. Let's just say they don't make many with figures like that."

Miles took a deep breath and let it out slowly.

So did the gentleman we were talking with.

It was kind of funny.

"I remember her," the man said. "She is hard to forget."

Miles turned to me. "See? I told you so."

"Knock it off," I told him. "No one likes a braggart."

"Doris," the man said softly. "Who can forget Doris."

It was more of a statement than a question.

"Yeah," Miles said. "That's right. Her name was Doris. Now I remember."

"Does Doris have a last name?" I asked.

"Yeah. Yeah," the man said. "Her name was Doris Schlumpnuts."

Schlumpnuts?! Was he *joking*?!

"That's right," Miles said with a wide grin. "It *was* Schlumpnuts!"

I stared at Miles. "You couldn't remember a name like *that*?!"

"It didn't fit her. I guess I *wanted* to forget that her last name was Schlumpnuts."

"It was her married name," the man said.

"So there was a *Mr.* Schlumpnuts?" I asked.

It was hard not to laugh.

I kept thinking about how kids were cruel. And could only imagine what they would do with *that* name! And how that name *alone* would bring on wedgies.

Stolen?

I wondered how often that poor kid was found stuffed in his locker.

And to think. A beautiful woman had married him *and* taken his name.

She *had* to love the guy!

I felt a little sorry for Doris Schlumpnuts.

I would have asked them where she lived. But to be honest? It would be easy enough to find them.

I mean, really. How many Schlumpnuts's could there be?!

Then the next thought hit me and I couldn't stop laughing.

I laughed so hard, I was bent over with pain.

"What's so funny?" Miles asked.

"I was just thinking to myself: How many Schlumpnuts's could there be?"

"So?" Miles asked.

"So then I had the thought… that there were at least two."

It took ten minutes before the four of us could stop laughing.

Chapter 11

We left the office where Doris used to work.

"So where to now, boss?" Miles asked.

"Would you stop calling me that?" I said as I pulled open the car door.

We both got into the car.

"I'll try," Miles said with a smile.

I could tell that he liked calling me that. Or maybe he just liked getting me riled up.

In the future? I'll have to try to not let it bother me.

"So where to now?" Miles asked again.

"Let's stop for lunch first. Then I'll look up the Schlumpnuts's in a phone book."

I'm sorry. Every time I said that name I

cracked up.

It was so wacky you'd *swear* someone made it up.

"So what do you like to eat?" I asked Miles.

He shrugged in his seat. "I'll eat anything."

"Burgers? Sandwiches? Pizza? Chinese food?" I asked.

"Yup. I like them all," Miles said.

He looked a little nervous.

I wondered why.

Then I think I figured it out.

"It's on me," I said easily. I didn't want him to think this was charity or anything.

I liked his company.

It would be nice to have someone with me while I ate. I was getting used to eating alone lately.

Too used to it.

It would be nice to have the company. *His* company.

I never liked eating alone. For many years I never had to.

Patti had been there for breakfast and dinner. I ate with co-workers or clients or the partners at the brokerage firm for lunch. So this whole eating alone thing was new for me.

Not that I was bad company or anything. But eating alone made my mind wander.

Usually it wandered to places that were, well, not fun.

"I haven't had Chinese food in *years*!" Miles said with feeling.

Years? That's a long time to go without Chinese food!

"Want to go today?" I asked.

"Sure," he said. He was trying to look casual. Trying to hide his excitement.

He failed. He was as excited as a little kid.

I smiled on the inside. I didn't want him to know that I knew he was so excited.

"Okay, then. Chinese it is."

We were far from Peaceville, and in a big town. They *had* to have a Chinese restaurant around town somewhere.

Stolen?

"Oh," I said pointing. "There's one."

Miles craned his neck to look.

"What's a Chinese buffet?" he asked.

"You've never been to one?" I asked.

He shook his head. "Nope."

I got excited about taking Miles to a Chinese buffet. The variety of food is amazing. And the fact that it's "all you can eat" will blow him away.

"You'll see," I told him.

I couldn't stop the smile that spread across my face.

"I hope you're hungry," I said simply.

Miles groaned. "I'm always hungry. Or so it seems."

"Well, we'll stay as long as you'd like," I said. "I'll bet you won't be hungry by the time we leave."

"I'll take that bet," he said. "You know what they say about Chinese food. Don't you?"

"That you're hungry ten minutes after eating it?" I asked.

"Yeah," he said with a grin.

"Well," I said. "They weren't talking about Chinese buffets when they made up *that* phrase."

I pulled into a parking space.

His deep laughter rumbled up from his chest. "I'll still take you up on that bet," he said.

I shook my head. "You'll be sorry you did. So I'm taking back my bet."

"Afraid you're going to lose, son?" he asked.

We got out of the car.

"I'd be cheating, Pops," I told him as we walked to the door.

I opened the door to the restaurant.

"See what a Chinese buffet is first. *Then* you can take me up on the bet if you want. But to be honest? It was a sucker bet. So I take it back."

I watched as his eyes looked over the buffet tables.

There was table after table of Chinese dishes.

"How do you know what you're allowed to take?" he whispered to me.

"You're allowed to take it *all*," I whispered back.

Chapter 12

We were almost finished with our meal.

Up until now, we were probably there for about an hour. Maybe more.

Miles ate the entire time. Nonstop.

"So?" I asked him. "What do you think?"

He licked sticky red sauce off his fingers.

"These ribs? Amazing!"

"And the rest of the stuff?" I asked.

"Amazing," he said.

I think he tasted every item on all seven tables.

He had exotic taste. He liked the squid. He *loved* the octopus.

I'm not into that stuff.

Give me a steak. Or some ribs. Or some crab

legs.

But you can keep the squid and the octopus.

I watched as he went back for more.

This time he was starting on the desserts.

He came back with a plate full of sweets.

"This is a treat," he said. "I don't usually get dessert."

"Well, eat all you want," I told him.

"This is amazing," he said. He bit into a piece of fresh pineapple. "I can't believe it all costs the same. No matter how much you eat."

"You might as well stuff yourself," I said.

I smiled at the thought. He sure was stuffing himself.

I went back for some ice cream. Vanilla.

They had some apple pie. But it didn't look as good as Hilda's.

I took it anyhow.

"Oh, that looks good," Miles said.

I cut a forkful of pie. I added a bit of vanilla ice cream. Then I tasted it.

Yup. I was right. I knew it wouldn't be as good

as Hilda's.

"It's not as good as Hilda's," I said.

"I'll have to take some. To see if you're right," he said.

He got up to get some pie.

When he came back, he had pie and about ten other items.

"You have a sweet tooth?" I asked him.

"Not always. But I do like a good dessert now and then."

"Try those little rolly cakes," I suggested. "The ones with the white cream. They're good." I pointed to the cakes I was talking about.

He popped one in his mouth.

"They're called jelly-roll cakes," Miles said.

I rolled my eyes. "Know it all!"

He shook his head. "No. Not really. My mother used to make them. When I was a little boy."

He looked off into space.

"Boy could she cook! She was a good woman, my mother," he said.

I signaled for the waitress.

"Yes, sir?" she asked. "May I get you anything else? More soda?"

"No thank you. Just the check, please."

"Was everything okay?" she asked.

"Perfect," I said. "Thank you."

"Yes," Miles added. "Everything was perfect! This place is great!"

The waitress smiled a pretty smile. "Thank you. I'm glad you enjoyed yourselves. Please come back again soon."

"Would you happen to have a phone book? An area phone book?" I asked her.

"Yes. I think we have one. It's by the cash register," she said. "I'll get it for you."

"Don't trouble yourself," I told her. "We'll look at it on our way out. Thank you."

I waited for Miles to finish his third plate of desserts. And his last bowl of ice cream. I think he had four. And he'd used the giant soup bowls. Not the tiny ice cream bowls. He'd scooped at least four flavors into each bowl.

"Had enough?" I asked when he put his spoon

Stolen?

down.

He smiled warmly. "I think so."

"Ready to go?" I asked him.

He nodded. "I guess so."

That made me laugh. "We *could* stay. If you want some more."

"I would love some more," he said with a chuckle. "But my pants are now too tight."

I didn't know how to respond to that.

He was grinning a devilish little grin.

"I *could* unbuckle. But out of respect for you, I won't," Miles said.

"Gee. Thanks." I grinned back.

We got up to leave.

"Thank you, Dan," Miles said seriously. "This was the nicest meal I've had in a very long time."

I nodded. "Thank *you*, Miles. It was nice for me too. You're good company."

He looked pleased.

We stopped at the register on the way out. To look at the phone book.

It was just as I'd thought. There were very few

Schlumpnuts's around.

"There's only one listed in the phone book," I told Miles.

"What's the address?" he asked.

I looked it up and wrote it down.

"I know where that is," Miles said. "I'll show you the way."

So we drove over to their home.

Chapter 13

"How long do you think it'll take to get there?" I asked Miles.

"About twenty minutes," he replied. "Maybe twenty-five."

I nodded.

We drove in silence.

I was trying to digest my food. I was stuffed.

It would've been nice to take a nap after that meal. I mentioned that to Miles.

"Yes, sir-ee. I agree," Miles said. "A nap would suit me well right about now."

We were quiet after that again.

Both lost in our own thoughts, I guess.

About ten minutes later I turned to Miles.

"So are you hungry?" I asked.

He rumbled with laughter. "No."

"See? You would've lost that bet," I said.

"You were right," he replied. "It *was* a sucker bet."

We laughed at that. And then it got silent once more.

A few minutes later, I spoke again.

"So what do you think you'll find?" I asked Miles.

"Excuse me?" he asked.

I reworded the question. "What do you think Doris will look like?"

"Still good. Maybe not as perfect as she once was. But a woman like that? They grow old well."

Miles smiled.

"Are you trying to picture her?" I asked him.

"No. I'm remembering her as she was," he admitted.

"That explains the smile," I noted.

"Sure does, son. It sure does."

We pulled up to their house about ten minutes

Stolen?

later.

It was a small house. Nothing big or fancy. But nice.

Homey.

Trees in the yard. Flower beds. White picket fence.

It was a nice home.

Tended with care.

"Are you ready for this?" I asked Miles.

"As ready as I'll ever be," he replied.

He smoothed out the wrinkles in his clothes as we walked to the front door.

I rang the bell.

It took a few seconds, but a woman answered the door.

This had to be Doris.

She was a knockout!

Sure, she wasn't young anymore. But she was everything Miles had said she was.

Pretty, classy, refined. And she had dignity.

I could tell by the way she held her head.

"May I help you, gentlemen?"

Miles spoke first.

"My name is Miles. I don't know if you remember me," he said quickly. "But we met a long, long time ago. At the junkyard. Where you and your husband brought his car. The Camaro. A '69 Camaro? Do you remember?"

He sounded like he was really nervous. He was talking too fast. His arms were flailing all around. And his voice cracked, too!

Here he was, a grown man—an *old* man—and his *voice* cracked!

How funny was *that*?!

This woman sure did do something for Miles. He was all wound up!

He went from zero to sixty in about half a second.

If it wasn't so amusing, it would've been pathetic to watch.

"Yes," she said slowly. "Yes. I *do* remember you."

He was beaming so brightly, I thought his face would crack off.

Stolen?

"Oh," she said with a soft sigh. "That was a day. Was it not?"

"It sure was a day!" Miles agreed.

"Please. Please come in," she said.

She stood aside so we could enter her home.

It was as picture perfect on the inside as it was on the outside.

Everything was neat. In its proper place.

The couch looked worn, but not shabby. It looked comfortable. Inviting.

Almost as if it really wanted you to sit on it. Like it welcomed you to sit down.

We sat down.

"May I get you some tea? Or some coffee?" she asked.

"No thank you," I said. "Not for me, thanks. We just had a huge meal."

I looked at Miles.

He was staring at Doris.

He looked like a thirteen-year-old. One who was in love. Not just love love. But *luv* love.

"I'd love to have some tea," he said. "But only

if you'll join me."

Her face brightened. "That would be delightful," she said.

Delightful? Who says "delightful" anymore? Doris Schlumpnuts says delightful.

And it seemed Miles was delighted that Doris thought his idea was delightful.

I wondered if *Mr.* Schlumpnuts would put a damper on this delight-fest.

Chapter 14

I waited until she left the living room. Then I turned to Miles.

"What are you *doing*?!" I asked him.

He tried to look innocent. "What do you mean?" he asked.

"You're not here on a *date*, old man!" I stated quietly.

His telling grin said it all.

"Would you *behave* yourself?" I pleaded. "We're here to find out about her husband's car. You remember her husband. Right? The man she's *married* to?"

If I could've burst his little happy bubble? *That* was what I needed to say to do it.

His face fell flat. He silly grin was wiped away in an instant.

"Oh," he said. "Right. Sorry. I forgot she was married."

He looked toward the door that must have gone to the kitchen. The door she went through to get the tea.

"She does something to me. Has a pull on me or something," he said slowly.

"She does have something about her," I had to admit.

"She's…" he tried to think of a good word to use. "Bewitching."

I had to smile. In this case? It certainly seemed as if that were true.

"Well, behave yourself, Miles. She's a married woman," I said.

If anyone knew how hurtful it was for another man to steal one's wife? It was me.

She came back into the room. Her hands were holding a tray.

Miles jumped up to get the tray.

Stolen?

"Please," he said. "Allow me."

He took the tray from her hands.

"You can put it on the coffee table," she said.

Miles bent to put the tray on the table. Then he looked over at me.

"Look, Dan. Jelly-roll cake!" he said to me.

I rolled my eyes. But then I laughed.

"His mother made jelly-roll cake," I told Doris.

"Oh, that's funny. It's my best cake recipe. Please try some, Miles. Let me know how mine compares."

I watched as Miles took a slice of cake.

Was that his *pinkie* sticking up in the air?

What had come *over* this man?!

I watched with disgust. But I also wondered how he would respond.

What if the cake was awful? What would he say?

I shouldn't have wasted my time wondering.

"It's as good as Mom's recipe," he said with a warm smile.

You'd think Doris had just won the Nobel

Peace Prize. She was glowing with pride.

"Why thank you, Miles," she said breathlessly.

She sounded a bit like Marilyn Monroe when she'd said that.

I looked over at Miles.

I think he was blushing.

It was hard to tell with his dark skin tone. But yes, I think he *was* blushing.

Someone needed another wake-up call.

"So is your husband home?" I asked Doris.

"No I'm sorry, he's not," she said softly.

"We need to get some information from him," I told her.

"Maybe I can help," she offered.

"It's about that car you brought to the junkyard," Miles said.

He took another piece of cake.

"That car!" she said with a little huff. "It's been *years*! But I'm still sick of that car!"

She wore a cute little pout on her face.

I had to admit, she was *way* too old for me, but she *was* adorable.

Stolen?

"Why?" Miles asked her.

She sighed heavily. But even that seemed cute.

"Well, you see," she started. "It all happened a long, *long* time ago."

She moved back in her seat. Wiggling around to get comfortable.

That gave me the feeling that this was going to be a long story.

So I sat back and got comfortable too.

Chapter 15

"You see. Sunny loved that car," she started.

"Who's Sunny?" I asked.

"Oh. I'm sorry. That's my husband," she said. "Sunny."

Sunny Schlumpnuts? The man's name is Sunny *Schlumpnuts*?

That *had* to have been made up!

"Anyhow. Sunny got that car when he was a kid."

"He must've been very proud of it," Miles said. He sipped some tea. Then put the teacup down on the saucer with a rattle.

Guess he wasn't used to using fine china. But who was?

Stolen?

"Oh, he *was* proud of it!" she said with feeling. "*Too* proud!"

I watched as she took a sip of tea. She moved with ease. Dainty and graceful. Fluid.

"*That's* what got him into trouble!" she said with force.

"Trouble?" I asked.

"Oh yes," she said. "*Big* trouble!"

She took a bite of cake. I didn't mind that *her* pinkie was out. Not as much as I minded that Miles still has *his* stuck out.

He looked ridiculous.

But I guess one does strange things when trying to impress a woman.

I'm sure I've done *my* share of strange things.

Good thing I was too in a fog when I'd *done* them to remember what they were!

"He thought that car was the best. *The* best!" she went on.

"It was a nice car, I'm sure," I said.

"Yes, but he thought it was the best," she repeated. "So he used to race it."

She looked at Miles and me.

"Sunny was a wild boy. A real handful. At least that's what his parents said. Anyhow. Sunny raced that car against all the other kids' cars."

"How'd it do?" Miles asked.

"Oh, he won all right," Doris said with a huff.

I felt there had to be more to this story, and waited for it.

"He won every race he was in. Scared his mother silly! But then a new kid came to town," she said simply.

That didn't sound good.

"This new kid was a real rooster. Crowing day and night. Said his car was better. Faster."

"And I bet Sunny didn't like that much," Miles said with a knowing grin.

She shook her head. "Like I said. That boy was a wild child! He didn't like it one bit."

"So what happened?" I asked.

"The new kid challenged Sunny to a race," she said. "But not just a race to see who was faster. No. This kid was mouthy. And slick. A city boy."

Stolen?

"What did he want to race for? Money?" I asked.

"Don't I wish," she said with a little huff.

She was getting upset. I could tell.

"No. This new kid wanted to race for pink slips," she said.

Pink slips?

I didn't get it. The only pink slips *I* knew of were what people got when they got fired. You know. Getting the pink slip.

"Back in the day," Miles explained. "The original car title was called the pink slip."

"Oh," I said. "*Now* it makes sense."

Miles winked at Doris. Then he shook his head and rolled his eyes. "Kids," was all he said.

Doris smiled.

"So, like an idiot, Sunny took him up on it. But Sunny was just a kid from a small town. He was honest and didn't know there were shysters out there."

Shysters. Now *there's* a word I hadn't heard in a long time!

Shysters were the norm now. It's what people were. Everyone out for themselves. Looking out for number one by ripping off everyone else.

Thanks to all the shysters we now have? We even have the saying: *Let the buyer beware.*

We have so many shysters in our midst, we *expect* people to be shysters! We *count* on it!

In law? Politics? Business? Most are shysters!

An honest politician? That's a rarity now-a-days.

And we don't spend our time worrying about *if* we're going to get ripped off. No! We worry about how *badly* we're going to get ripped off.

Getting ripped off is now a *given*. (Just think about the price of gas or your phone or cable bill!)

"The other boy had a trick up his sleeve," Doris said with anger. "A trick that would *guarantee* that he would win the race."

Chapter 16

"He raced for the title of his *car*?" I asked with shock.

She shook her head with sadness. "He sure did. He was young. And stupid."

"So what happened?" Miles asked Doris.

Doris snorted a laugh. "What do you *think* happened?"

"Sunny lost?" I asked.

She grimaced and nodded. "He sure did."

She reached for the teapot that was sitting in the center of the tray she'd brought out. Then she refilled Miles's teacup.

"The kid used nitrous oxide. You know, NOX. It gave his car that extra shot of energy to win the race."

"Sunny didn't know about NOX?" I asked.

"Not before that race," she said with a sad smile.

"But I bet he knew about it *after* the race," Miles stated.

Doris nodded. "Yes he did."

"But wait," I said. "He must have had the car for years after that. Didn't you bring it to the junkyard many years later? From what Miles said, Sunny wasn't a kid when you guys brought it to the junkyard."

She nodded again. "That's when all the trouble started. You see, Sunny *loved* that car. He had expected to win. If it had been a fair race, he *would* have won."

"So what did he do?" Miles asked.

She shook her head and laughed. "He ran. Left town. Took off like a bat out of hell."

That made us laugh.

"He was scared out of his wits. If you asked me? I'd tell you he was scared senseless. Because that's what he did. He did something senseless. Just took off. Left his family. His school. His friends," she explained. "He even left me."

"Now *that's* senseless," Miles said with a grin.

Doris smiled prettily at him. Then she quickly looked down at her cup of tea.

Her old face was a deep pink.

Oh. Great. Now *she* was blushing!

"Well, he called his family. To tell them what had happened. And he called me, too. To say he was sorry," she said shyly. "And then he said he'd send for me. When he was ready to get married. He promised."

He'd obviously kept his promise.

"A few months later he sent me a train ticket."

She was smiling with the memory.

"So what happened afterwards?" I asked.

"We got married and worked hard. We bought this house. Had a daughter. You know. Lived our lives," she said with a shy smile.

"Did you ever go back home?" Miles asked.

She shook her head. "No. Never. Not as long as

we owned that car. Sunny was too afraid."

"That was a long time ago. And he was a kid. Why was he still afraid?" I asked.

"Because the kid who won the race? He became a lawyer. Not just *a* lawyer. He became the town lawyer!"

"So?" Miles asked.

"So, he vowed to find Sunny and throw him in jail for not handing over the car."

"But the lawyer guy had *cheated*!" I said with anger.

"He didn't see it that way," Doris said softly.

"Why didn't he just track Sunny down?" Miles asked.

"Yes," I said. "How hard could it be to track down a man named Sunny Schlumpnuts?"

Again, I couldn't say the name with a straight face. I started laughing.

"Sorry," I mumbled to Doris.

She rolled her eyes.

"Don't apologize to *me*! I *know* it's totally absurd!" she said.

Stolen?

"Why didn't the lawyer find you?" Miles asked.

"We found you easily. Within minutes," I added.

"Because Sunny's name isn't Schlumpnuts. It wasn't Sunny, either," she told us. "He made up the name so he wouldn't get caught."

I *knew* it! I *knew* that it had to be a made up name!

"Of all names to take! Why did he choose *Sunny Schlumpnuts*?!" I asked Doris.

Chapter 17

"His first name was Donny. But he had a real sunny personality. So people here started calling him Sunny. That name just stuck," Doris said.

"I meant his last name. Why did he chose his *last* name?!" I asked.

"Oh. Right," she said with a giggle. "I'm so used to it now. I don't even notice it any more."

I found that hard to believe.

But I guess someone could get used to *anything* with time!

"Donny had a sense of humor. A quirky sense of humor," she explained. "He figured who would make up the name Schlumpnuts? And furthermore, who would take *on* that name? No

Stolen?

one! Not if they didn't *have* to!" she added.

She had a good point.

But still. His plan was moronic.

But if you think about it? A teenage kid in a heap of trouble? Yeah, he might come up with such a plan.

I guess he hadn't had much time to work out all the kinks. And to be honest? There were *many* kinks in his plan.

In fact, his plan was so stupid, it wrapped around to genius.

"So is that why the VIN numbers were scratched off?" Miles asked.

She nodded. "Yes. He didn't want anyone to be able to trace the car."

"So after all of *that*, why did he bring the car to the junkyard?" I asked.

She looked at her feet. Ashamed. "It was my fault. I was jealous of the car."

That was just… silly. I mean, I was jealous of Neil. He's the guy who ran off with my wife. But a *car*?

I needed to ask. "You were jealous of a *car*?" I asked her.

She smiled wanly. "He gave up *everything* for that car. I thought he loved it more than me."

She must have realized how silly that sounded.

"I was young too. And in love," she said thinly.

"Why didn't you just make him *sell* it?" I asked.

"He refused. He didn't want anyone else to have it. She was his baby."

It was weird, but it made sense. Sort of. In a weird, obsessed way.

"He made a deal with Junkyard Dan thirty years ago," Miles said. "Sunny made Dan promise not to sell it. Not for as long as Sunny lived. I was there. I remember."

My cell phone rang. "Hello?"

"Hey, Dan. It's me Bubba. Look. I hate to tell you this, but you've got another problem."

"Now what?!" I said with frustration.

"A customer came in while you were gone."

"So?" I asked.

Stolen?

"So, they were looking at an old 1930 Ford Coupe," he said.

"So?" I asked again. "Did you sell it to them?"

"No," Bubba said.

"Why not?" I asked.

"Um, we came across something weird in the back of the car," he explained.

"So?" I said. "Throw it out. Bury it. Or burn it. What's the big deal?"

"It's a machine gun," Bubba said simply.

I exploded. "A *what*?!"

"A machine gun!" he said louder.

"I *heard* you," I said. "I just couldn't believe my ears."

"Well, believe them. What do you want me to do with it?"

How was *I* supposed to know?!

"I can't deal with this right now," I told him. "I'll catch up with you when I get back home."

"Okay, Dan. I'll see you then," Bubba said.

"See you then," I said.

I hung up.

All of a sudden I was very tired.

"Problems at the yard?" Miles asked.

"What else is new?!" I responded.

I turned to Doris.

"Look. I have a customer. A father who has a teenage son. He's losing his son to girls, friends and cars. He wants his son back. Wants a little more time with him before the kid grows up and leaves the nest. He wants to buy the Camaro. Wants to restore it with his son."

"Is that why you're here?" Doris asked. "To ask permission to sell it?"

"Well, I didn't know about the deal. I had to make sure the car wasn't stolen. You know, because of the scratched off VIN numbers."

She nodded in understanding.

"You think Sunny will let us sell it?" I asked.

Chapter 18

Her eyes darkened. "Sunny passed away last year."

I was shocked. I wasn't expecting that.

"I'm so sorry for your loss," I said.

"Thank you," she said softly.

I watched as her eyes filled with tears.

"Want to hear something funny?" she asked. She started laughing through her tears.

There was a box of tissues on the end table next to me. I handed her the tissue box.

"Thank you," she said.

She dabbed at her eyes with a tissue.

"On his deathbed. Do you want to know what his last words were?" she asked us.

I didn't know if I wanted to know. But it seemed impolite to say no.

"Sure," I told her.

"His last words were: *I regret making Junkyard Dan promise not to sell the car. No one else ever got to feel the joy of that car. No one but me. That was selfish of me.*"

Those were the last words of a man to his *wife*?

Those were the dying words of a man who made his wife give up her hometown and family because he'd done something stupid?

Maybe she had a right to think he loved that car more than her.

Not to mention that he'd named himself properly. He really *was* a "Sunny Schlumpnuts!"

This was a bizarre story.

I didn't know how to respond to it.

"So you think we can sell it?" I finally asked her.

She shrugged. "I don't see why not," she said with a smile.

Oh. Good. So this was working out well.

Stolen?

"I'll go get you the VIN number if you want it," she offered.

"That would be *great*," I said happily.

This was working out *very* well.

The ride home was a happy one.

"You did good back there, boss," Miles said.

"Would you stop calling me boss?!"

My phone rang again. I saw it was Bubba's number.

"What now?!" I barked into the phone.

"Hey, chill out, dude. Roger came over with his son. They're here. At the garage. Any word on that VIN?"

"Yeah. I got it. Tell them to meet us at the yard. We'll be there in about fifteen minutes."

When we pulled up, Roger and his son were sitting by the front fence.

I unlocked the gate and we all walked over to the Camaro.

"So? What do you think?" Roger asked his son.

"This'll be *great*, Dad! Thanks! A first gen

Camaro?! These are *amazing*!"

It was all rusted out and falling apart. It sat for almost three decades in the hot sun. Fading and rusting.

"It'll take a *lot* of time to restore it," Roger said to his son. "Think you'll have the time?"

The kid looked at the Camaro. I could tell he was seeing it not for what it was. But for what it could be. What they could make it become.

"Don't worry, Dad. I'll *make* the time!" the kid said.

Roger Strands looked at me and smiled. His face was glowing with happiness.

My job here was done.